This one is for you Jayden, thank you for making my world a better place.

-Love MOM

Jayden, 4-years-old

Jayden
Won't Go To Bed

By T.L. Derby

Jayden Won't Go to Bed
Copyright © 2017 By Clear Fork Publishing
Artwork Copyright © 2017 By Tannya L. Derby

Summary: Jayden is four and like any four-year-old he doesn't like to go to bed. In this story he does everything to avoid going to bed all the while his mother is reminding him and moving him through the process of getting there. Jayden runs around playing while his mother rounds him up. Finally, Jayden takes things into his own hands and hides from his mom and while hiding the inevitable happens.

Clear Fork Publishing
P.O. Box 870
102 S. Swenson
Stamford, Texas 79553
(325)773-5550
www.clearforkpublishing.com

Printed and Bound in the United States of America.
ISBN - 978-1-946101-94-5
LCN - 2016955120

Clear Fork Publishing
www.clearforkpublishing.com

Jayden is four
and he loves to play.

He plays and plays until
he hears his mom say.

"It's time for bed, it's time lets go.
Get your blankets and your bear,
it's getting late you know."

Jayden runs up the stairs
and into his room.

His mother opens
the curtains to show
him the moon.

"It is time for bed, my dear little Jay.
It's time for bed, time to hit the hay."

She takes him softly
by his hands.

He takes a bath

and puts on his jams.

He brushes his teeth

and combs his hair.

He runs past his mom and
heads down the stairs.

"Jay, it's late,
it's time for bed.
It's time to rest your
sleepy head."

Jayden runs to his toys
and throws on his suit,
the one to fight fires

in his hat

and his boots.

"Jayden, it's enough, it's the end of the day. It's time for bed, put the toys away."

"I won't go to bed this night or the next. I won't go to bed. I do not need rest."

Jayden takes off back up the stairs.

He climbs on her bed and hides from her there.

She enters the room and looks down at the bump.
"It's time for bed my dear little lump."

"Let's read a book then rest our heads and
snuggle down in our nice warm beds."

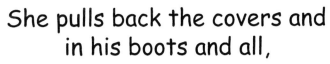

She pulls back the covers and
in his boots and all,

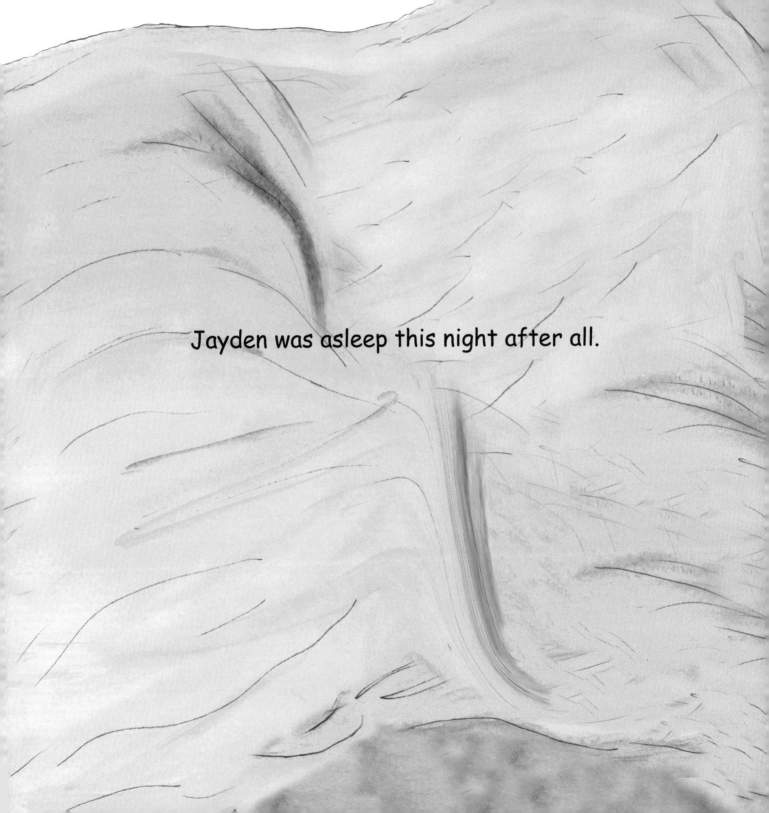

Jayden was asleep this night after all.

Tannya L. Derby

I am a children's book Author and Illustrator. I have found my love for writing and art is my joy in life so I made it my career. Now I help others to make their dreams come true. I am not only educated with a BFA in Creative Writing for Entertainment and an MFA In Creative Writing. I am also an autodidact in illustrating, screenwriting, and painting for over 20 years.

My love for art and writing began in my childhood with drawing and painting pictures with my mother and writing small stories. As a child's book author and Illustrator, I am able to incorporate my artistic ability and my writing skills together to create a life long career of magic.

I am also a published poet of "Trying Hard to Understand" and "Dance the Dance." In November 2015, I proudly published my first book, "Joy of Sisters" which was a personal project.

Having my art and writing studio in my home, I am surrounded by the love and support of my wonderful husband Todd and our children, which makes it easy to enjoy the work I do.